I0692162

THE ADVENTURES OF ABIGAIL AND WALTER:

Just The Way We Are

Story By Melissa Frederick

Illustrated By Lori Lay

DEDICATION

To The Lord above for giving me the ability to follow my dream.
To Jared and Ethan for the love and inspiration that only children can bring.
To the other two members of Sweet Darlin's, Billie and Lori, for making me part of something better than I ever could be alone.

The Adventures of Abigail & Walter: Just The Way We Are

Manufactured in the United States of America

Abigail & Walter: the first book of their adventures.
Text copyright © 2016 Melissa Frederick | Illustrations copyright © 2016 Lori Lay
Published by BMF Publishing, LLC | Billie Blankenship | Lexington, NC

ISBN: 978-0-9960328-3-4

CONTENTS

ABIGAIL

Abigail was glad to leave the house today.
Everyone else was finishing chores and it seemed
as if the entire house was turned upside down.
The twins were looking everywhere for matching
shoes. She truly did like it when her cousins came
to visit but they liked to stay inside and it was
nice to get out and feel the sun. Feeling the warm
rays against her wings always made her smile. It
made her happy. Floating on the wind, landing
on the pretty flowers made her feel invisible.

She enjoyed being surrounded by all the different colors of the world. That's how she met Walter. Her eyes were drawn to the color of a pretty red rose. It was so beautiful it almost made her eyes hurt.

Abigail Rose Stone. That was her name. She thought it made sense for her to be especially fond of roses since she was named after one. Bursting from her cocoon when she smelled the sweet scent. Funny how she could remember that smell even as the memory of her broken leg was just a dim recollection.

Her mom said she broke it because she was in such a hurry to SEE the rose and not just smell it!

It didn't seem odd to always fasten on a belt either. She had to have something to hold her cane so she could fly. It was just another part of her morning routine, like washing her face or brushing her teeth. But when she got close to the rose that day she saw a lady bug under it, taking a deep breath.

That was Walter and he loved the smells of the garden almost as much as she did. And the colors! Today the flowers were especially bright because there were rain clouds in the distance.

The sun glinted off her glasses as she raised her face to the bright light of the morning. Sometimes, she thought, I feel so free that the wind could blow me wherever I want to go, without ever having to move my stiff leg at all.

PRETENDING

Today she was going to play pretend. It was one of her favorite games. I am going to be a leaf, she smiled to herself, that twirls around and around and around and then I'm going to let myself fall down…down….down…

Until I land on a cushioned flower petal.

Her mind felt free as she put her dreams into action.

Spinning...Spinning.... Spinning. Like being on a carousel

that never stopped. Later I am going to be a famous painter,

she thought.

Others can come from miles around to see all the

wonderful colors I put down on paper. I will bring the world

to life. I can have an art studio so the whole neighborhood can

appreciate the beauty. And Walter, well Walter could be her

manager. Her eyes sparkled as she thought of what Walter

would say about that!

Mmmmmmm. Or maybe I can just be a princess today.

She tilted her head as she thought aloud, "If I gathered some of the stems from several daylilies, I can make a crown!

And my cane can be a regal staff used to anoint all my knights.. I bet the baby ants would enjoy that". Walter of course would have to be the head of the guards. Abigail giggled. She could just see Walter as he tried to protect her from intruders to the castle!!

Today, as she was flying, she saw her friend Walter half hiding under a clump of grass.

She hurried to him. She could hardly wait to tell him about the plans for her crown. Maybe they could go play by the old wooden fence and make him a sword. She hurried along.

Walter was her very best friend in the world. He understood her like nobody else ever could. And he loved her just the way she was.

WALTER

Walter was on his way to meet Abigail. They shared so many adventures together. He was eager to tell her about the new rock he had just found last evening.

It was all sparkly and shiny just peeping out from under the rusted old tin can at the edge of the garden. He knew Abigail loved to play pretend. He couldn't quite imagine what they could do with this pretty pebble but he knew Abigail would find something. She always did.

It was nice to have Abigail as his best friend. Abigail knew that he didn't always like to fly. She didn't mind walking beside him sometimes, even though it made it a little harder for her to get to where she wanted to go with her stiff leg. Walter never minded walking because he was kind of roly-poly.

Sometimes when he was flying very high it was hard for him and he couldn't look down. And if anything landed on him, like a drop of rain, he just knew it would make him crash to the ground.

He wasn't afraid of the heights really, it's just that sometimes it seemed scary to be so far above the rest of the world. Usually he would walk and Abigail would dance around in front of him in the air. She was always so excited with her hands frantically waving as she described what they were going to do next. Always full of ideas for adventures they were going to share.

The way he waddled and the way she walked made a really good pair as they strolled along between the flower stalks.

Abigail loved to fly because it was hard for her to walk but she did it for him. She knew how he felt about being so high above the ground. Abigail was the best. He was walking now as he hurried to catch up to her.

SAM

Just as he was turning the corner around the old garden hose, Sam, the cricket was coming out of his log.

Maybe he should start flying now he thought to himself. Sam was always mean. Sure enough as soon as Sam saw him, he started coming toward him pointing his finger at him. "Walter is Heartless!! A heartless Onespot that can't fly straight!!" cackled Sam.

And then he started laughing. Again! He was always laughing at Walter.

It was a mean laugh and the sounds of his laugh would ring around in Walter's head and make him shrivel up inside. He didn't like being laughed at and called names.

He wasn't quite fast enough though. He hurried along as fast as he could while pretending it didn't bother him. He could hear Sam taunting him as he rushed past.

"Onespot!! Heartless Walter!"

He was breathing hard by the time he got to a clump of grass at the edge of the garden.

He was completely out of breath. He just sat down. He wasn't excited about the pebble anymore. Sam made fun of everything about him. His size, his color and sometimes even his name.

Maybe Sam was right.

What kind of ladybug was he anyway? Maybe he couldn't fly straight. He had never actually seen himself fly. And his one spot did look like a heart. He crawled under a blade of grass and just started crying. The big fat drops made a puddle at his feet. He cried so hard a baby ant starting crying too, upset at the loud noisy sobs he made as he gasped for air.

RAIN

Abigail was past the field of sunflowers before she spotted Walter crying.

"What's wrong Walter?" said Abigail.
"Why are you crying? I can barely see you.
Are you hiding from me?"

It took several minutes before Walter could
stop crying long enough to answer.

"When I came outside my door this morning I thought I could smell some rain. You know I
don't like the rain when it hits my open wings. So
I decided to walk to come meet you today."

"But Walter", said Abigail all confused.
"You should not cry because of rain. Rain makes
the flowers grow because they get thirsty. Rain
helps the gardens."

They had this conversation before. Abigail did not like it when the rain hit her wings either. But she loved the brightness the world became when it was over.

"It wasn't the rain that made me cry Abigail. It was Sam! That mean cricket that lives under the log next to the tallest sunflower."

Abigail knew all about Sam. He tried to make Abigail cry too. She often wondered why others seem to take pleasure in hurting those around them. Her grandmother, Nomi had told her that sometimes it was because they hurt inside themselves.

But that didn't make it any easier when they were laughing at you.

"Do you remember what I told you my name was Abigail?" said Walter. Walter was proud of his name. His daddy told him he came from a long line of handsome ladybugs.

"My name is Walter Thomas Edwards the Third! When Sam saw me walking", continued Walter, "He laughed at me. He was calling me names! He said I was not a real ladybug. He started calling me HEARTLESS and ONESPOT!! He could tell that I am different"

At this Walter started spurting out a fresh batch of tears.

"What do you mean Walter? Why do you think you are different?" Abigail could not quite understand. Walter looked normal to her.

"Abigail!!" Cried Walter. "Don't you see the huge black spot on my back? "

"Yes, what's wrong with that? My Mom has two spots one on each of her wings."

"But I am not a butterfly Abigail!! Don't you see? I am a ladybug! Ladybugs are supposed to have spots all over their body. But I don't."

"I only have this one huge black spot."

"MY NAME IS WALTER THOMAS EDWARDS THE THIRD not ONESPOT!!!" Walter sobbed. "He was laughing, snickering behind his hand at me. I'm not heartless Abigail!! Really! Truly! I'm not!!"

FRIENDS

When Walter started crying again Abigail could barely understand what he was saying. She flew over to where he was hiding underneath a blade of grass. She thought Walter was beautiful.

He was a bright shade of red with one big

black spot on his back. It was shaped like a heart but she thought that was pretty. She knew other ladybugs had many spots but even some of those had them in different places on their body.

She still did not understand why Walter was crying but he was her best friend. So she wrapped her wings around him and started crying too.

They made quite a pair. With the way Walter was almost but not quite hidden under the blade of grass and the way Abigail's wings fluttered as she cried, they looked like a vibrating rainbow.

Walter looked up through his blurry eyes and said "Why are you crying Abigail?" If there was one thing in the world that Walter hated to see it was Abigail crying. She was always so strong and happy.

"Because you are my friend. And I don't like to see you sad. Is being called Spot a bad thing? Maybe he was trying to give you a nickname."

SPECIAL

Abigail knew Sam could be mean. She had heard him laugh at some of the small, younger crickets. But she wanted to cheer up Walter.

So she reminded him of her nickname.

"Remember my nickname that daddy gave me, Walter? You laughed when I told you he calls me Dinkin. He says it's because I'm small and special to him. Maybe Sam was trying to say you were special. But it was not nice of him to laugh at you. I don't like it when people laugh at me either. That's mean."

They had stopped crying now. Walter just sat there and tried to explain. He thought Sam was right. He didn't think he was special at all.

"But he was right Abigail. I'm supposed to have more than one spot."

"The only other markings I have are when I open my wings. See?"

At this Walter spread his wings wide just as if he was going to jump in the air and fly. Abigail knew Walter did not like to fly very often. When they did go places in a hurry she was always in front leading the way.

BEAUTIFUL

"But Walter that's beautiful," cried Abigail. She was still sitting on the ground and could see what Walter could not. It was amazing!

She was so surprised she had never seen it before.

"When you spread your wings open wide I can see what looks like a giant W. Don't you see Walter. You have beautiful spots. You ARE different. But being different is good. The letter W stands for a lot of good things. Like.. Wonderful.. I think you are wonderful.. And wise.

When you grow up that letter W will show people that you are wise. Like my grandmother Nomi. She knows everything! But most of all W stands for Walter. And that's your name. You are so special God put your initial on you! You have the perfect name. I love you just the way you are!"

Abigail spread her wings and started dancing around in the air. She was laughing now. Walter landed on the ground again and watched as Abigail spun around in the air. He was unsure what she thought was so special about that and truthfully he had never really noticed before. Not even before he went to bed and had to wash all his feet.

"Really? Do you think that's special?" asked Walter.

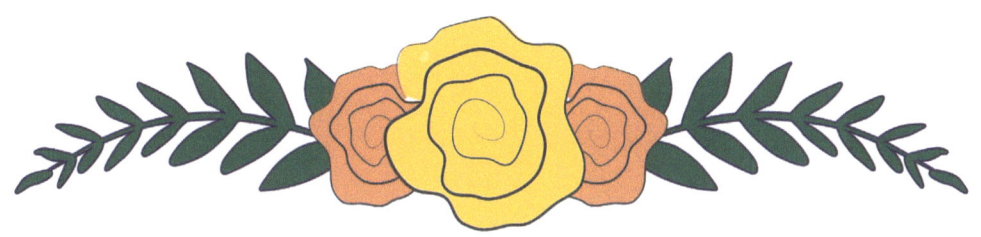

DIFFERENCES

"Yes, I do" replied Abigail. "My mama told me that everybody is special. She said everybody was different because that's how God made us. Look at Annie and Alice. They are twins but they each have their own unique nature. They are not the same person even though since they are twins they look a lot like."

Annie and Alice were Abigail's cousins. They were a few years older than her and always seem to be getting into mischief, according to her grandma Nomi. That was just fine with Abigail.

If everybody was watching what Annie and Alice were doing, they had less time to wonder about Abigail's adventures.

As she thought of this morning's episodes when shoes seemed to be flying by themselves, she laughed even harder. She was laughing so hard it was hard for to fly. She came back down beside Walter and almost hit the ground.

"Daddy says they are like two peas in a pod. He said we needed to tie a ribbon around one of their feet so we can tell them apart. One should be pink and the other should be purple.

Wouldn't it be funny if they did that and then they switched ribbons?" That was something she could just imagine Annie and Alice doing.

LAUGHTER

Abigail was laughing so hard that she had tears coming out of her eyes again. Abigail love life but when she cried her whole body shimmered. She laughed so hard she had to wrap her arms around her tummy to keep from falling over.

Seeing Abigail starting to fall over made Walter start laughing too.

He forgot about his tears as he thought about what Abigail said. He was special! And the next time Sam laughed at him or called him names, he was going to proudly tell him so!

They laughed so hard and so loud that Mr. Mantis heard them and almost started laughing himself. As a retired music teacher, he believed children were a special blessing.

"What has you children cackling so hard" he said as his hands came unfolded to rest on his hips.

But Abigail and Walter couldn't stop. They were giggling uncontrollably.

They started flying and twirling in the air, dancing above Mr. Mantis's head. The lavender bush he was perched on shook in the breeze as they flew by. He just wiggled his antennae as he smiled. He marveled at the sound of their laughter as it echoed through the garden. Bright and carefree.

"Look" screamed Walter as he soared above the daylilies, stretching his wings wide.

"I am Walter!!"

"Don't forget wonderful and wise" giggled Abigail.

THE END

BULLYING

Bullying is when one person is being mean to another person. This can mean laughing at others or calling them names when they are not like you. No two individuals are completely alike.

We are all different. That makes us special. It makes others special too.

ABOUT THE AUTHOR

MELISSA FREDERICK, *The Author*

Melissa, although a health care worker by trade, is the daughter of a farmer that loves nothing more than wiggling her toes in the dirt as she coaxes flowers to bloom. Unless it's floating between the kitchen and sewing room!! Bringing to life tantalizing aromas from the oven or arranging a kaleidoscope of colors in a baby quilt soothes her soul. If the sound of children and animals playing together stream through an open window on a light breeze she considers herself to be in paradise.

LORI LAY
The Illustrator

Lori is a Graphic Designer living in North Carolina with her husband and their dog Waffles. When she's not working her day job she's trying new recipes (preferably ridiculously Southern), painting pet portraits, jamming out to 70's hits and decorating her house with giant penguins around the holidays. She loves the Blue Ridge Mountains, shopping local, the ocean, mermaids, the great outdoors, Autumn and all things art & design.

BILLIE BLANKENSHIP
The Publisher: BMF Publishing, LLC

Billie is a dedicated mother. Not only of her daughter but also of all the adults she interacts with as a geriatric nurse. Her sweet smile and soft voice charms even the most cantankerous patients into following her lead. But this West Virginia girl has a passionate nature. Her drive and determination allowed her to single-handedly start up her own publishing company. Make no mistake this soft Southern girl has a backbone of steel.

TOGETHER THEY ARE THE SWEET DARLIN'S

Sweet Darlin's is a unique trio of talented ladies that use their common yet diverse background to collaborate their special talents. Joining together they each contribute ideas, emotions and time to a myriad of different projects. We hope you enjoy these adventures as much as we did while creating them.